THE SINS OF A MAGE

AATMIKA KAPOOR

manda Publishers x BENZAITEN PRESS

Title: The Sins of a Mage

Author: Aatmika Kapoor

ISBN: 978-93-6402-066-4
Price in INR: 299/-
Manda Publishers
www.mandapublishers.com
publish@mandapublishers.com
+91 9999190496

Cover Image: Tanya
Typography: Siddharth

Distributed by:
Amazon, Flipkart, Manda Publishers etc.

Printer:
Manipal Technologies Ltd.
Noida

Benzaiten Press
An Imprint of Manda Publishers

DEDICATION

This novel is dedicated to all of the teenagers out there who are emotionally and mentally struggling and need the comfort of knowing they are not alone. Sometimes life has some bittersweet moments, but things always get better at the end. Learning to trust the future will bring happiness is of course hard, for anyone, but it's important to keep going. We all need to learn to embrace our imperfections, because every imperfection is absolutely perfect. I hope this book allows readers to see some similarities in behavior while reading how the characters interact with each other and their thoughts. Special thanks to both of my parents and my older brother for always being there for me whenever I needed it, and to my closest friends for giving me their ear when I need to ramble on about an ongoing topic in my life. Love you guys loads!

Table of Contents

THE BEGINNING

She was trembling, and her hands were shaking vigorously. She couldn't believe her eyes, nor comprehend the series of events that had taken place. Her mind had drawn to a blank, and there was a tremendous amount of terror visible in her eyes. Her breaths started getting louder and heavier with each exhale. She knew she had to run away from the horror, but her legs weren't obeying her mind.

The monster, with blood smeared all over its face and claws, had approached the young girl, eyes filled with fearsome menace. Even after going on a murderous rampage, the wild beast still had a voracious appetite for more. What more could it possibly want? It slowly came closer to Enola, licking the blood off its knife-like claws. Although Enola was unable to run away to potentially save her life, she was able to scoot herself backward just a couple of feet. Enola was on the verge of accepting that her life was going to end at any moment, when suddenly, she heard a swift movement from behind the monster. The monster and Enola broke their gaze as the beast turned back. There was nothing, just pitch silence. But of course, the ignorant beast took a few steps in the direction of the noise. After turning its neck left and right sharply, almost like how mums make kids do before crossing a road, the monster concluded there was nothing there. It had completely ignored the broken twigs on the floor, and a villager's head peeking out from one of the trees.

Moments later, there was an attack. Villagers, who had climbed high on the sequoia trees, jumped down on the wretched creature, stabbing it with freshly sharpened arrowheads made out of obsidian. The villagers, completely unaware that this creature had been alive for over 1,000 years and would not be affected by a stab wound, continued to attack the creature. Enola took advantage of the distraction, got up, and started running. She looked at Amapola, who had given her a slight nod of approval to run away. She ran as fast as she could, faster than ever before. The poor, unfortunate villagers had misjudged the beast, because seconds later, after the attack, the beast had aggressively shaken off all the people off his bulky back and thrown them to the ground.

Once it saw that Enola was no longer on the floor, which was covered in withered sepia leaves, it grunted in frustration that it had lost its prey, and decided to walk slowly, inspecting every direction for a sign that the girl may still be nearby. Enola, still running, looked back occasionally to see if the ugly monster was in hindsight. It wasn't. She took a well-deserved break, rested her back against a tree, and took deep and heavy breaths. She took advantage of this moment to recollect her thoughts. So much has happened to her, and the thirst for water was much desired, but in a forest with little to no streams, this was difficult to acquire.

Suddenly, Enola heard a noise, a noise she recognised very well, a faint growl. It sounded like a lion when it came into close contact with a deer. Instantly, it clicked. She knew what had just approached her. She took a deep sigh, accepting her fate, and fearfully looked up. It was the beast, its beady eyes staring straight at her. It took a great leap, claws in the air, mouth open to devour, with a stance of each limb opened wide, AND!

I shall stop there before you close the book with confusion written all over your face. Let me introduce myself. My name is Dresden Gandalf, and I live in the Aequcurin Kingdom. I am a mage, well, a mage in training. Lord Vaerlon says I'm too insensible... whatever that means. As a future high-council mage, I am often in the grand potions lab on the top of Morphil Hill, learning to make potions like how to make monkeys fly. It's very annoying and tedious. If you thought being a mage is fun and cool, you are very, very, very wrong. It is nowhere near being fun. It is quite possibly the worst job to have in all of Azadia. I would much rather have a job as a Dragon Caretaker, which, by the way, if you don't know, they have to clean up dragon faeces, than be some stupid mage. Lord Vaerlon is calling me right now. I'll explain everything to you later.

BACK TO ME

Ok, I'm back. Just another day for another useless potion-making session. Who is ever going to use a potion to make an armchair into a cup of coffee? Like, what? Before I explain the horrific first few paragraphs of the first chapter, I would like for you to know me first, and how my life has been for the past few days. I am the son of the highest mage, which means I have to learn how to make such potions. I utterly hate all the high mages. They have all kept unachievable expectations and unbearable tasks for me to complete daily. I just want to be a normal person. Why must I have to face all of these responsibilities? It is not fair. I never wanted to be born into a prestigious mage family.

And to make my situation even worse, my older brother, Kironin, had already completed all his training to be the heir of our father when he was my age. Which basically means I'm behind schedule. I was expected to have finished my training by now and compete in a grand duel with my brother to see who would be the heir of my father and be the next High Mage of all the High-Council Mages.

For those who don't live in Azadia and don't know what a grand duel is, it is a competition between two or more male heirs to the King, and they must fight in a series of events. Each event is held at the end of the week for five weeks, which gives the other days in the week to train. However, each event is slightly altered for more than two competitors. If the High Mage has only one son, then the grand duel is unnecessary.

The first event is a sword fight. First to land a touch three times will lose. Of course, each son wears heavy metal armour, so no impact is made on their bodies, but the swords are real. In typical Azadian fencing, contestants normally don't wear headgear, as landing a touch in the head area is off-bounds and an immediate elimination from the event or, depending on the severity of the injuries, possibly the entirety of the duel. I know I am for sure going to lose that match.

The second match might kill me before I even attempt the other three events. Now, you might be aware of bullfights. However, we don't have bulls in Azadia, so we have dragon fights, which are a tad bit worse, considering that a dragon can burn you alive and turn you into ash, or they could drop you from a high altitude. Thankfully, there are special mouthguards cast with a spell making them indestructible and placed over the dragon's long snout, similar to muzzles dogs wear, but I could still fall. The objective of the event is that each competitor is given a large golden egg and is meant to protect it throughout the games. This event takes place high up in the shimmery sky, where riders are given a large staff that has a wire curled into a circle attached to the end of it. There are large podiums with rooms at the top where supporters from each side spectate the event. Whichever son can grab their rival's egg the greatest number of times within ninety minutes wins the event.

However, the third match was the worst. Each opponent will participate in a race with thirty-pound weights on their body. Fortunately, you are given free will to decide how you will divide the weight on your body. Previous opponents have either attached a fifteen-pound weight to each of their legs, and/or to their arms, or the full thirty pounds on their chosen limb.

The fourth event is probably the best event out of them all, because it is a contest to see who makes the better wooden ship in two hours. The requirements for the ship are that it has the Azadian flag carved into the front of the ship, it can hold ten or more glass coins, and it can float for ten minutes with the weight. I know I will be able to come up with a successful design, the only issue being that I can't build. Hopefully, my assistant, Alfonzed, will be able to do most of the building while I instruct him on what to do.

The last and, thankfully, final event of the grand duel is the most frightening event of them all. The oldest opponent is allowed to pick what kind of competition they want to compete in. I'm certain my older brother will pick an event that will surely end my life.

And the cherry on top is that each day after my torturous potion-making training, I am taunted by my displeased father about my progress. My father would walk to our lush, peaceful garden, which was an exquisite display of flora, and would often find me doodling in my notebook. The garden was my sanctuary of serenity because of how it nurtured calmness and was a place to reflect. The serene environment surrounded this majestic water fountain, which glistened in the bright sun and played nature's melodies.

I often spent much of my time in this haven of tranquillity to express myself through art. Art is uncommon among people who are meant to be eloquent communicators and beacons of knowledge. To do art was a symbol of disrespect to my father because it showed my lack of interest in what is meant to be my line of work. On my father's usual walks to our garden, he was never surprised to see me doodling in a brown sketchbook gifted to me by my great-grandfather, but was rather disappointed. It's not my fault I don't want to become a high-council mage and take over for my father. I never asked for any of this.

My dream is to be an artist, not a distinguished high mage. I have tried many times to enlighten my father that I am on this journey of self-discovery, and need to continue expressing myself creatively. He will never understand. He only cares about who shall rule our kingdom next, and if they proceed to work hard to accomplish my father's lifelong dream of making Aequcurin the most thriving kingdom in Azadia.

But instead of having the opportunity to pursue my dreams, I am resentfully tasked with a job to make sure my father's dream, who doesn't care about mine, is achieved, and burdened with expectations to be just as amazing, and just as much of an embodiment of perfection, as my older brother is. Life truly is unfair.

WHAT?

Suddenly, there were two knocks on my door, followed by a deep and resonant voice that said, "Prince Dresden, your father awaits you in the grand potions lab for your final exam. Please be punctual."

No one else in the kingdom has a voice as low as Lord Vaerlon. And of course, I need to take an exam, an exam I was not even informed about, how lovely. I made my way down my windy staircase, and headed towards our large gates, with ten guards on each side. The two guards opened and closed the gate for me. After a brief five-minute walk outside my home, I arrived in the village town square, a local market with street vendors selling all of their specialities. Young kids love markets like this, giggles and laughter echoing all over the area, and small shadows flitting past vendors and carts. I walked past them all, dodging all the hyper children who must have eaten far too many sweets, to a stone path that led to the top of Morphil Hill to meet up with my stern, and slightly pessimistic, father.

After opening the intricately carved timber entrance, I made my way up the elegant spiral staircase and reached the grand potions lab, along the corridor to the right, third door. I took deep breaths and turned the knob. There I saw the most aggravating person ever, Empusa Dwade. Mrs Dwade is notorious for her almost-impossible-to-pass exams. But of course, my perfect-in-every-way-possible brother passed it with an almost perfect score. He got points docked because he unfortunately wrote his last name initial instead of his full name.

"Good morning, Dresden, excited to take a test?" said Mrs Dwade in her extra-chirpy voice.

"Good morning, Mrs Dwade. Excited, no. Nervous, yes," I responded, slightly stuttering because of how concerning the smile on Mrs Dwade's unproportionate face was. Every time I saw her, she was always smiling, as if the smile was super-glued on.

I grabbed my black cloak from the coat rack which stood beside the entrance. After putting it on, I slowly walked over to my desk, where different potions and ingredients were kept in front of me. I was very confused, I had thought my exam would be a written test, not practical. My chances of failing this have slightly decreased now.

"We shall now begin your final exam, which concludes your training."

"CONCLUDE YOUR TRAINING! WHAT!" I thought I was severely behind. I am terrible at hiding my emotions, so as soon as I heard Mrs Dwade say that, my father was able to notice my furrowed brows and dilated pupils.

Hence, he said, "Son, I have thought long and hard about your training. I believe you are ready. After completing this practical exam, you and your brother shall begin training for the Grand Duel, which will take place in a few days," and concluded his shocking news with, "Good luck!"

My father walked out of the room to help me concentrate while Mrs. Dwade was instructing me on the directions.

"To start off simple, please take this paper towel and turn it into a cup of black coffee."

This was an interesting request, but easy enough. I grabbed the jar of Elixir of Dark Waters due to its natural abundance of transforming chemicals. But to turn the matter itself into a completely different state, I would need a few leaves from the Plant of Disruption. I took three dried leaves from the plant, and I began to grind it until it became a fine powder. By making it into a powder, the elixir can correctly combine the molecules to create a substance that allows the transformation to happen. I dropped three drops of the elixir into the bowl where the fine powder sat, and slowly mixed it in, careful not to disrupt the process. Once the powder and elixir had created a paste-like texture, I scooped it up and gently spread it across the paper towel. The spell had already begun twelve seconds after applying the paste. Within moments, Mrs. Dwade had received her cup of coffee to keep her energised and awake throughout the rest of the exam.

Mrs Dwade was holding a clipboard on which I assumed my results would be written, but after completing the first task, Mrs Dwade scribbled something on her clipboard, and said, "That will be all, you may exit the testing room now."

"That will be all"? I thought there was more to the test. I was sure there was more to the test. After that first simple question, I had anticipated that this exam wouldn't be too difficult to pass. Everyone knows that turning a paper towel into a cup of coffee requires three dried leaves from the Plant of Disruption and three drops of Elixir of Dark Waters. It was merely common knowledge. But an exam that decides my future is only one simple question? Seems like a mistake. Surely Father is aware that my future as a potential high-mage utterly depended on this exam. Now I am aggravated that I was forced against my own will to take this test, but at least make me take it correctly. Sometimes I just don't understand my father's way of thinking. What was the point in making me train my whole life to take an exam consisting of one singular question?

Dreadful News

Once I left the testing room, my father and Mrs Dwade were discussing my execution of the potion, and how well I performed it. Since the two had taken four hours and twenty-seven minutes to grade it, and that the exam was merely one question, I began to become worried, contemplating my life decisions and thinking I had done something wrong. Had I screwed up the first questions so badly that they couldn't test me on anything harder? My mind was creating "what if" scenarios, horrible ones too, and kept me restless.

I kept thinking about the exam as I walked back to my room. I had been in such deep thought that I was completely unaware of my surroundings. Likewise, I almost crashed into three street vendors, and a couple of boisterous children. Everyone who had taken a look at me walking had confusion written all over their faces. Once I reached my room, I took off my brown satchel, which held my imperial pen, an inkwell filled with a special Azul Ink, and my drawing notebook, and took off my thick black coat. I sat on my bed and rested my head on the backboard. I just could not stop thinking about it. I replayed everything that had happened in my head, hoping that I would remember anything to help me understand why the exam was only one question. So many people have cautiously informed me that Mrs Dwade's exams are one of the most difficult and mentally draining, yet my exam was one simple question. I was expecting her to ask me about the formulas to change substances into different forms of matter only using one chemically changing ingredient, not a question that anyone could answer. How does asking me such a question help prepare me to take over the throne one day? On that note, how does any of my training help me? When our country is at war with a rival, how does knowing that monkeys can fly if you make them drink a potion made of a few drops of the Vial of Flight?

After waiting for what felt like an eternity, Lord Vaerlon finally approached my bedroom. "The Royal Highness requests your presence in the Grand Ball Room to discuss matters regarding the exam you have recently completed."

I then proceeded to walk down the windy stairs and into a meticulously decorated corridor. On the walls surrounding the corridors hung monumental canvases with intricate portraits painted on them of former high-mages. Around each painting was an opulently designed frame with regal gold leaf accents and elegantly carved edges. They were frames that could only be found in a handful of locations. The entire corridor was brightly lit with about a dozen chandeliers. The Grand Ball Room was the seventh door to the left, so it was an awful long walk.

The Grand Ball Room was used to host events such as galas for my father to flaunt his success and make everyone in the room jealous. I was often held hostage at those galas, against my will, and forced to be mature. Of course, there wasn't any sight of children my age. There was no one to socialise with, except the adults who were almost or more than twice my age. My brother had no issue talking to folks he didn't know, regardless of their age. He has always been great with words and knows how to entertain any audience. According to Lord Vaerlon, my speaking is of a soft-spoken individual whose words often linger in the air like a gentle breeze, barely breaking the silence. That was a delicate way of telling me I am a shy speaker.

After almost murdering my legs with that walk to the room, I arrived in the ballroom to see my father in his oversized throne-like chair, upholstered in rich velvet and plush cushions, inviting you to sink in and experience a sense of luxury and comfort. He was seated with perfect posture, his hands gracefully resting on his lap, with a serene expression, exuding an air of confidence and poise. With shoulders back and head held high, stood Lord Vaerlon beside my father. In order to match their distinguishes, I immediately straightened my back, and strode forward at a steady pace.

I started the conversation with a simple formal greeting, "Hello Father, and good evening."

Although I am horrible at talking to people, I am able to read their facial expressions quite well. I couldn't quite make out what my father was thinking, but I am sure it's a complex emotion. His face was sown like an intricate tapestry of emotions, woven with threads of unwillingness and slight sorrow.

"Good evening, son," replied my father in his stern voice. "You are well aware that the exam you recently took will have a great impact on your future, and will decide the future of Aequcurin. Now you may be wondering why the exam was only one question, well, son, you see," he took a deep breath and continued, "I don't have much longer to live."

Frozen in place, my eyes wide and unblinking, a look of disbelief etched across my face as if the weight of the world has suddenly crashed down upon me. Tears streaming down my cheeks, I stood pale and trembling, struggling to process the heartbreaking reality that had just unfolded. My father, dying? How could this be possible? So, the exam wasn't because they thought I was ready to compete in the Grand Duel, it was to quickly figure out who the successor to my father would be.

My father broke the awkward silence by reading my mind and saying, "Hence, you will have to participate and engage in a thrilling competition against your brother. Your training begins next week."

He began to speak softly, almost like a whisper, his words dripping with hope and longing for understanding when he said, "Please do not tell your brother of this matter."

I madc a slight nod and exited the room. I am not one to display any sort of emotions. I had not made the slightest expression at my mother's funeral, but for some odd reason, I felt the need to cry, the need to release all my emotions. I knew the waterworks were going to begin at any moment, so I quickly scurried to my bedroom and shut the door so no one would see me at my lowest.

My mother passed away when I was just six and a half, and although I was aware of her death at such a young age, I still didn't feel the need to cry. I don't remember her much except for her luscious, silky, brown hair, soft hands, and her blue eyes. My brother and father would often recite stories to me about how lovely she was, and how she was supportive of every decision made in our family. It made me wish I remembered her. But my father gave me everything. He created so many opportunities for me to thrive and flourish, and I feel as if I have taken advantage of those. And now he's leaving me. Forever

My Torturous Training

I cried myself to sleep once I reached my room. I simply could not comprehend it; my mind wouldn't let me accept it. When I woke up, it was late at night, and I saw a plate full of supper left on my desk. I suddenly realised how long I had been sleeping, and slowly got up. I pushed aside my quilted bed cover, designed with intricate patterns and soft hues of pastel colours, and put on my sleeping loafers, which are like a warm hug for your feet, with soft, plush fabric that feels like walking on clouds, making every step feel cosy and comforting. The food was still warm, which gave me an indication that it must have been around an hour after dinner ended. I sat in my chair and ate my food peacefully, thinking about all the moments I shared with my father, and trying to accept his fate, which I could not be able to alter.

After a while, I began thinking about why my brother was unaware of my father's upcoming death. I expected him to be told this matter first, rather than me. I thought about this for some time. My brother is far more trustworthy than me. But then it occurred to me that my brother may not want to participate in the Grand Duel knowing my father's death is near.

The Grand Duel! The training begins in a day. Oh no, oh no, oh no. I'm going to utterly fail. I began to panic just at the thought of it. I was more than confident that my brother would be declared the winner of the competition. Although I was certain that my brother would win, a part of me hoped I had a chance to prove myself worthy, a chance to possibly make my father happy.

The sudden motivation filled me with newfound energy, eagerness to transform my hopes into reality, and a sense of readiness to tackle any challenges coming my way. I knew then and there that I was going to succeed... maybe.

I finished eating and went back to sleep, thinking about all the new strategies I could use against my brother and imagining how to come to a glorious victory.

I woke up the very next morning, energised to seize the day and prepare for my battle against my brother in a few days. The first event requires one's core, arms, shoulders, back, and chest strength to be extremely strong to successfully manoeuvre the sword around to the desired target. After having my morning meal, I headed down to the armoury and met with my instructor, Jean-Philippe Boulet, who will be intensely training me this week. Sir

Boulet has a thick French accent, so most of his speaking sounded like this:

"Today vee vill begin our leçon with a very quick verkout, so let auss start."

I gestured with a simple nod.

"Our leçon shall consist of thérty reps ov plank holding for von minute and ve vill end ze verkout vith sïxty reps ov side plank holding for deux minutes."

I gestured with another uncertain and hesitant nod because I hardly work out and couldn't understand his heavy French accent. This also doesn't seem like it is going to be a "quick" workout.

3 hours later

That was not a quick workout! I nearly died before even participating in any events, and we haven't even begun today's training.

This might be a good place to pause for a moment and assure the reader in every instance in which English is spoken in a French accent in this story, it will not be in the kind of ham-fisted attempt at portraying a French accent like the preceding few lines. This is the last instance in which it will occur.

Monsieur Boulet started teaching me fencing with an épée, a sharp-pointed duelling sword, designed for thrusting and used, with the end blunted, and explained to me what an *en garde* position was and when used at what point in time during the matches. I probably understood less than half of what Monsieur Boulet was saying, but I would have to try harder to understand to win this first event and make my father proud.

Each day onwards, I continued to train, and with every ounce of strength I had, I pushed through the pain, determined to beat my brother and prove to everyone my worth.

The Shortest Grand Duel

I woke up bright and early the day of the first event, looked at myself in the mirror, and gave myself a quick pep talk before heading downstairs to have my morning meal. Once I arrived in our grand dining room and seated myself in my chair, three butlers came to my service. One had tied a napkin around my neck to ensure any and all food spills would not stain my clothes, one filled my glass with fresh orange juice, and one brought me my meal. And of course, my brother is already done with his breakfast, so I had to eat alone. I usually eat alone, but on that day, I hoped to eat with someone for a change.

So I sat there all alone, trying to think of different ways I could strategically parry in order to win this event. I thought about the moves he might make and how to properly defend myself while simultaneously trying to get a point. In my head, I created about nineteen scenarios in my head and used all the advice that Monsieur Boulet had taught me. And just like that, I was prepared for the event.

I headed back to my room to start wearing my armour and gathering my sword when there was a knock at the door. It was once again Lord Vaerlon. He wanted to inform me that there were thirty minutes until the event was going to start. Keeping that information in mind, I resumed putting on the heavy armour and quickly warmed up some of my sword moves and tactics I planned to use, which I think the judges would find quite pleasing. I tried my best to push all of the nerves to the back of my head and stay confident but not cocky, by diverting all my thoughts to the scenarios I made and simply concentrating on those.

Time had gone by so fast that it felt like a few seconds until I heard another knock on the door by Lord Vaerlon to come downstairs and head over to our playing field, dedicated to hosting events such as this. After walking what felt like a mile to the sidelines, I started warming up once again, trying to exhale out all the nerves that no longer remained in the back of my mind. Lord Vaerlon was also at the sidelines next to me, bombarding me with phrases to motivate me, which helped a little; I tuned out most of what he was saying and was rather trying to make out how my brother was feeling, who was on the opposite side of the field.

That's when I saw a referee run to the middle of the field with a microphone. Referees in Aequcurin are quite different from the referees you may be used to seeing on television. Rather than wearing black athletic shorts and a striped jersey with a whistle hung around their necks, referees are usually wearing a black robe made out of the finest leather, with gold accents on the cuffs of the sleeves and the collar. "Ladies and gentlemen, today marks a glorious occasion where the two sons of the High Mage Slawoki Gandalf will compete in the Grand Duel, a competition created to determine the next successor of the High Mage," began the referee, kindling some enthusiasm amongst the audience. "Our first event will be a sword fight. The objective is to land a touch in the opponent's target area three times to win the match. The game will end once a player reaches three touches first, hence there will be no draws. Enough with the talking, folks, let's now call in our players to the centre of the field."

This was my cue. I jogged to the centre, trying not to use much of my energy but simultaneously not trying to look slow in front of the thousands of people in the packed crowd. Instead, I looked at my brother, attempting to read his extremely hidden expressions. While doing this, I had tuned out but returned to my senses when I heard the referee scream "GO!" into the microphone.

Kironin had gotten into position, and so had I. My brain began to recite all the advice Monsieur Boulet had given me throughout that week of training: "Make sure you are always on your toes so it's easier to move to block and attack your opponent swiftly," and, "Keep certain muscles loose and others tight, such as your core," while also giving myself some pep talks.

I then lifted my toes, moved around a little, and raised my sword while lunging onto my right leg. I took deep breaths, slowly starting to forget all the scenarios and plans I had made, as the nervousness took over my mind. I tried brushing it off, but my brother had made a strike to my chest, to which my quick reflexes came in and blocked his hit. Now I could only focus on the match and how to better judge Kironin, rather than the plans that have officially left my brain.

Because my brother attacked first, I had exactly one minute to get a touch; otherwise, my brother would receive his first point, which gave him "priority." After the block, I pushed away his sword and executed a well-timed attack on his stomach that he wasn't prepared for. That's when I heard the scoreboard above us make a "Ding" sound and the crowd's unison cheering. The glorious first point had now belonged to me. My brother grunted a little, and I could see the slight shock on his face as he must have underestimated me.

We both got back into our starting position, waiting to see if anyone would start the match. I knew I had gotten an easy point, and the rest of the matches wouldn't be like the first one. I decided to start the match and attack his right arm when I was going for his chest again, but Kironin quickly dodged that and went for my right arm. I raised my arm, and his sword went under my forearm, completely missing my arm. This was my opportunity to strike again. I gripped the handle of the sword again and scooted backwards so my attack could be perfect. Unfortunately, my brother had realised the attack I was planning to make and immediately blocked it, giving him a chance to strike a point. To confuse me, he started shifting his feet left and right and moved his sword closer to me and then toward him. I couldn't tell when he was going to strike, so I decided to do the same thing. In doing so, my brother was able to see a pattern within my movements and swiftly moved towards me and hastily stuck a point in my left arm. A similar but slightly different "Ding" had been played, and the scores were now tied.

Our third match had begun and lasted around the same time. At this point, I was starting to see all the new ways my brother was using to trick me to gain a point. So, although this match lasted the same amount of time as the previous one, there was more action going on, as both of us started attacking and blocking faster, desperate to gain the second point. In the end, I had managed to get the point by using an uncommon trick Monsieur Boulet had taught me, which was manoeuvring the wrist in a certain way, pretending to strike a point in one direction and at the last-minute strike somewhere else to confuse the opponent. I was honestly surprised with myself because I thought I wasn't going to last very long in this match. All I needed now was one more point, and the victory in this match would belong to me. Suddenly, overconfidence had taken over me, and it was getting harder and harder to block and attack simultaneously. My brother had already gotten his second point in less than three minutes.

Now begins the final match, the match that will decide the winner of the first event. My heart began racing, and the beats started getting louder and louder. I closed my eyes, trying to recollect my thoughts and calm myself, but all I could hear was my unsteady and rapid heartbeat, and this little voice at the back of my mind telling me how I could potentially mess this up. I opened my eyes and started concentrating on my brother's expression. I noticed my brother avoiding eye contact, leading me to suspect that he too was incredibly nervous.

I started the match fairly well; I blocked all of his hits and attempted to make my own. I got close to striking a point as well, but I unfortunately miscalculated the hit and missed him barely. Just moments later, the unfairness began. I had used another technique taught to me and stuck a point on him. It must have been quite light, because my brother continued playing. Confused, I wasn't able to keep up with his attacks, and he had hit me hard on my collarbone. No one had seen my point. My confusion turned into aggravation quickly. My brother was declared the winner of the event. The referee ran to the field with his microphone and a gold medal.

"That was quite a match," the referee began to say. "Both sons showed exquisite sportsmanship and effort while competing, and for that could we all give them a great round of applause." The crowd cheered so loudly that my eardrums were almost about to pop. That helped me sort of forget the fact that I was meant to win, but I came to my senses after the crowd's screams had dialled down. The referee continued to talk about how our performance was when he finally took the medal and put it over my brother's neck. This is exactly the point where my anger had reached its peak. Because I am the son of an important figure, I had to control my overwhelming urge to speak my mind and just release all the anger I was experiencing. This single event had truly solidified my mentality of, "Life isn't fair."

One Stupid Mistake

How could they? How could they just let him win? I had won fair and square. I trained for so long, an entire week of utter torture, and they just let him win? I thought that I had gotten the last point to break the tie, and yet he still won. I couldn't fathom what had happened.

Usually, I wouldn't act like this if he had won, but I won that last point, and I deserved the win, not Kironin. I wanted to forfeit the whole duel, knowing the spectators would continue to cheat and give my brother points he never made.

Once I ran back to my room from the playing field, I threw all my armour to the ground, knowing I would never need to use it again. I am not going to compete in something that is rigged. Justice must be served.

That's when it hit me! The only way to get justice is revenge. I, of course, didn't have the guts to tamper with any of my brother's equipment, so I decided to take a less interactive route, and instead do something with a greater chance of succeeding and is more invisible. I opted to cast a spell.

With this idea, I hurriedly dashed out of the room and into Lord Vaerlon's sleeping chambers. There, I knew he had kept a special wand carved with intricate designs, a spell book filled with intriguing spells from various categories, and a helpful glossary at the end that would be of much use to me, as I have never cast a spell before. I snatched both items quickly and headed back to my room.

My fingers danced over the pages, flipping them with urgency, each page a whisper of ancient knowledge, as I hunted for the incantation that could change everything. "Ah ha!" I exclaimed after finding the perfect spell. I carefully picked up the wand, looked at myself in the mirror, took a deep breath, recited the incantation to the best of my ability, "Enolakim", and flicked the wand the way the book instructed me to.

After executing the spell, I looked back into the mirror and could no longer see my reflection, only a small young girl. I started to feel my chest getting heavier. This was the moment that I realised I had made a grave mistake.

The Two Best Friends

"C'mon, Enola, hurry up, or we are going to be late! I can't get another tardy, or Mrs Zooperloud will give me detention," yelled Nish from the bus window. Enola rushed around her house, trying to find her PE clothes, hopeful to not get a zero in her participation grade for a non-dress. At last, she found them from under her bed, stuffed them in her already packed backpack, took a quick look at herself in the mirror to make sure she had worn her outfit correctly and no unwelcomed strand of hair was out of place, and ran through the door to meet with Nish, her best friend. Nish and Enola have been friends for about a year now, and they've always been close. Two peas in a pod are what everyone called them. They've tried to keep their friendship a secret, so people don't get the wrong idea, but it is hard to stay away from your best friend.

Enola has always been the quiet one, while Nish has always been the jokester. From all the time they have spent together, Enola has slowly started to open up more to him and talk a lot more, but only with her close friends. By spending time with Enola, Nish has learned to stay quiet and observant in tense situations, rather than cracking up a joke and displacing the atmosphere of the room. He is the kind of guy who goes with the flow of life and sees what happens. However, when it comes to his social life and relationships with others, he becomes a different person. His personality goes from nonchalant to being altruistic and overprotective.

Once, an insecure jerk named Bryce, but everyone called him Bagpipes due to his horrible saxophone playing, had come up to Enola and started to rant about how disgusting her face was, covered with acne, to which she needed makeup to cover it up, and made fun of her petite height. Nish witnessed it all. Without any hesitation, Nish struck Bryce's face with his fist and gave him a well-deserved black eye. But Bryce didn't back down. He had no sense of empathy whatsoever. He believed in his hurtful words. Unaware of Nish's seven years of karate training, Bryce attempted to uppercut his face but missed because Nish had already blocked him with his forearm. Nish was just about to strike again when a yard duty from behind came running, grabbed a hold of his arm, and pushed him to the side. The same yard duty grabbed both of Bryce's arms and inspected his injury. After sending Nish to the principal's office to discuss a suitable punishment for his act of justice, the yard duty walked Bryce to the nurse's office.

Our principal, Mr Grashop, otherwise known as Mr Gregarious due to his outgoing and overly social

personality, and his smile which never leavcs his face, had gotten a message through his walkie-talkie, that all the staff carry around. Mr Grashop is known for his light punishments, regardless of the offence, because he is a strong believer that people can change and learn their lessons.
Soon after arriving at the office that belonged to the person with the most authority in the entire school, Nish's breathing pattern had increased drastically, and his heartbeat was quite rapid. Nish had never gotten into trouble before and has tried to stay out of huge conflicts. His emotions got the best of him; he couldn't stand someone saying insulting remarks about his best friend. She meant the world to him, and he wasn't going to let this slide.

"So let me get this straight: Bryce was using harmful language with Enola, so you punched him in the face," said the slightly confuzzled principal, trying to understand what had happened.

Nish gave a slight nod.

"I see... I will talk with Bryce and teach him a lesson with my words and not actions. As for you, pick up ten pieces of trash tomorrow during lunch and make sure you apologise to Bryce."

See what I mean about light punishments? Nish was relieved to know that all he had to do was pick some trash up, and not get a referral or detention.

Enola has been receiving comments from Bryce for a while. She's tried to confront him about this but loses her confidence and begins stuttering, giving Bryce another opportunity to make fun of her. He's constantly stealing her things, calling her things he should not be calling her, and doing anything to make her frustrated and annoyed. Nish is only aware of half the things he's done. She can't risk him knowing.

This is why, when Enola finally got on the bus to sit next to Nish, she had to put on a fake smile and act like everything was OK.

The entire bus ride was quite pedestrian; the two friends just sat next to each other and disclosed many reasons why they disliked certain individuals. It was normal for teenagers to share things like that. Enola has never been good at hiding her feelings, it was a known fact. Within two minutes of their conversation, he had already noticed her scratching her nose multiple times, and her voice had gotten softer — all signs of her hiding something. One other thing to know about Enola is she is not good at opening up either. So, there is no point in asking her if something is wrong, because all she is going to respond with is, "Nothing, everything is fine," and try her best to put on a smile that seems genuine. Half of her smiles weren't genuine. She just could not forget what had happened to her. It was all so abrupt. The minute she starts Year 8, people start looking at her differently, calling out her insecurities, and making her feel like she isn't welcome anymore. The only person making her feel better was Nish.

Nish is an only child. He has always been occupied with work from his numerous extracurricular classes and his abundance of school work. Enola has always felt bad for him. He keeps reassuring her that he can tolerate his workload, but she knows him too well to know that he is simply lying to himself.

Once the two got off the bus, they went their separate ways because they knew if anyone saw them together, everyone would start to get the wrong ideas and stop considering them as just friends.

If you are still confused, turn the page and I shall make you less confused. **BIDIBIDI BOBBIDI BOO!**

YOU ARE SLIGHTLY LESS CONFUSED NOW... MAYBE

Anyway, you are probably still confused, maybe a bit less than when you read the first chapter. You might have noticed that the girl escaping the monster from the first chapter reappeared in the second chapter, only there wasn't a monster in the second chapter, and have slightly familiarised yourself with Enola. I think this calls for another introduction.

Enola Elizabeth lives in the suburbs of Winstoor, Strautus, in a normal-sized two-storey house, decorated with traditional Indian furniture, with a weird colour scheme painted on the walls. She has a younger sister, Avi, who has been her best friend for the longest time and spent every second with her, and an older brother, Kian, who has been someone she's looked up to all her life, hoping to be as perfect as he is. Her room has never changed since birth, so the walls are painted with a baby pink, with childish stickers stuck everywhere. Throughout the years, Enola has collected any letter or item to remember certain meaningful events and taped those to her wall. She calls it her "Wall of Memories". If you wrote and delivered her a letter or made her a drawing, it is probably going to be on her wall. Her parents are aware of everything in Enola's room, except for a secret diary hidden underneath many books and random scraps of paper in her chaotically organised bookshelf that no one knows about. Well, I know about it, and so do you, but no one besides us. It's our little secret, so shhh and don't tell a soul, or else. I am just kidding; I won't do anything... or will I? Because you hardly know me, I perhaps should not be scaring you, which is my cue to continue making you less confused. Enola's secret diary, which is blue with a vibrant sparkly E on the front of it, contains all of her secrets. Secrets even Nish doesn't know, and they share everything.

Ever since Enola was around five or six years old; her mother had enrolled her in a piano class. Ever since that day of her first lesson, she has never been able to let go of the piano. However, technology these days is starting to change the minds of these young individuals for the worse. Hence, Enola's slight decrease in passion for piano and increase in passion for her phone. She despises practising but doesn't dislike it enough to leave it.

Especially because she has been doing it for so long, it feels wrong to leave it now. So, she still plays it and practises an hour before her lesson or whenever she feels like it.

Another hobby Enola has developed, which she is actually passionate about, would be dance. Dance is an extremely common activity amongst girls of Indian descent, but to do two different styles is rare. She does Bharatanatyam, which is a traditional graceful form of dance originating from Tamil Nadu, and Bollywood, which is quite an energetic and aggressive dance style. Her dancing reflects her personality; she can be graceful around people she likes, and aggressive and mean around people who have nothing nice to say.

From the end of fifth grade, Enola was in desperate need to find a new hobby because she was starting to get a little bored with her already existing ones. She begged her father to consider enrolling her in a figure skating class after being completely mesmerised by the Olympics. Finally, her classes had begun, and now ice skating was something Enola never wanted to leave. As of today, she can gracefully execute complex, challenging, and impressive skills with her unyielding resilience. After doing figure skating for about three years, Enola has learned to be patient with herself and to take a moment to properly understand the technique to do the skill with the correct precision and elegance.

With all the information I have just provided, you might see yourself in Enola and relate to her. Unfortunately, Enola is a victim of horrible things and her so-called "perfect" life will be ruined by one stupid mistake. Her life will collapse within moments and she doesn't even know it.

The Uncovered Secret

It all started in the first week of 8th grade, and Enola was on a mission to make a good impression on her teachers. With all the quality time spent with Nish, Enola has gone from being diffident to becoming a social butterfly. So, to make a good impression with her new teachers, Enola was on her best behaviour to be as quiet as possible, regardless of how many friends she had in a class. Enola's schedule this year was a little disappointing because she didn't have any periods with any of her other close friends, but at least she had one period with Nish. Enola wished she didn't have any periods with him, because she was keeping a dark secret from him. But she knew she could never tell him it, because his heart would break in a million shards and may never recover. Her parents had finalised their decision to move Enola to a new school. The high school she was meant to go to was extremely difficult to pass, and to do extracurricular activities for college applications to stand out. Enola has known about this plan to move for a while now, and it's been killing her. As each day goes by, the closer the move-out date is. Enola was trying to slowly isolate herself from Nish so that when she left him, it wouldn't affect her or him as much. Out of all the days in the year, the day she would be moving out would be on 9th March 2025, Nish's 14th birthday. Nish's birthday gift would be her leaving, what a great and thoughtful gift. Enola has attempted to talk to her parents about this because she really didn't want to. Leaving everyone she loved emotionally crushed her soul and shattered it.

When Enola had made her way to her first period, which was her French 2 class, her plan had already failed. One of her friends, Mabel, had run to her, arms open wide, and squeezed the death out of her, but in a good way. Not many girls were taking French, so to reunite with someone she was relatively close with was a bit heartwarming and exciting to see someone with such high energy distract her from her secret. Mabel is a professional talker and occasionally trauma-dumped on Enola at the most random times, giving Enola a hint that she is considered trustworthy. Enola suffered from trust issues because she was betrayed by a person, she considered to be one of her closest friends. Knowing that someone trusted her enough to share their trauma was healing for her mind. Madame Béatrice hadn't made a seating chart for her students, so Enola and Mabel decided to sit together, and they made sure to be far from Nish. Mabel had thought the two had a fight, which is why Enola wanted to be away from him which worked well because she respected her decision.

The rest of the period was fun because Madame Béatrice had organised fun French games to help us warm up our brains and hopefully remember everything we learned the previous year. With everyone enjoying themselves, no one noticed the time, when all of a sudden, the bell rang. Time for Enola to go to American Revolution history class. Enola has never had any interest in American history and much preferred World History. Unlike Madame Béatrice, Mrs Barnes was extremely organised and knew exactly what she wanted to say and get done. When Enola walked into the heavily decorated classrooms, on the projector, she saw a seating chart categorised by students' first names. After taking a minute to figure out which seat on the third table would belong to her, she quickly spotted one of her friends, Jenny. Jenny was a tall, Asian girl with short but thick, black, glossy hair who was extremely intelligent. Enola made a small wave to her as she was getting out her pencil case and binder. Within moments of Mrs Barnes talking about her expectations and policies, Enola already knew that her class would be very boring and easy to pass.

Her next class was accelerated maths, which Enola was excited about because maths was her favourite subject. The teacher, Mrs Ahn, was well-educated and humorous and made learning Algebra 1 enjoyable to learn. All summer, Enola had been training her brain with challenging maths, so when the first unit on simple one-variable equations came along, Enola was prepared. Mrs

Ahn had arranged all the students in rows based on their last names, so when Enola sat in seat #7, she was greeted by many of her extremely talkative friends. This is where Enola's mission really falls apart. Enola hardly learns anything in maths, and so many of her friends surround her, Enola would not stop talking. But fortunately, Mrs Ahn was a lenient teacher and didn't mind the talking. Enola had a good feeling about this class.

The real trouble began when the bell rang, and Enola knew that during the passing period, she would spot Nish. Therefore, she decided to walk to her fourth period with her friend Valerie and meet up with her boyfriend, Bryce. At this point, Bryce hadn't done anything to Enola, yet, but instead annoyed her frequently. First, it started with small things like just calling her short and making fun of the way she walks and talks. She had been tolerating him for the whole week, up until he started stealing things off her backpack when she wasn't looking, which really upset her. Enola lacked confidence, so she decided to talk to Valerie about what had been happening to her. Valerie normally is extremely sweet and understanding, but sometimes she becomes biased towards certain people. Without hesitation, she took Bryce's side and told her, "Boys will be boys, what can you do?" Completely ignoring the fact that he was legitimately pissing her off, Enola gave up telling her what he has been doing and decided to take matters into her own hands. She had stopped talking to him and looked away every time he tried talking to her.

Enola's fourth period was meant for her to learn about forces and motion and Newton's three laws of motion, but was rather spent as a period to devise new plans on how to handle Bryce. Enola's fifth period was PE, and usually for the first week of school, the coaches never had anything planned, so the students would sit on the floor of their gym and socialise. Although Enola and Bryce had different PE teachers, during this first week of school, students were allowed to meet up with other students regardless of their teacher or grade. Therefore, Bryce and his friend made it their sole purpose to annoy Enola, ignoring her clear discomfort. Enola had to suffer for 45 minutes, every day, for a full week with Bryce. Telling an adult about Bryce would make her a snitch, so she tolerated it. In all her other periods, Enola was a bit sad when the bell rang, because it meant she had to leave some of her friends. She was thrilled when the bell rang after the 45 minutes of torture. Finally, she made her way to sixth period, English. English has never been Enola's strongest subject, but she loved writing, even if it wasn't great quality. She just loved expressing herself through the art of writing and found it a great therapy. That's why she has a hidden diary filled with all her feelings, rather than keeping them bottled up.

Her entire first week was a rollercoaster Enola never wanted to be on. Each period, she was a different person because of the different people there. In French, she had to distract herself from the fact that Nish was there, while in history, she distracted herself with books and classmates from the boring lessons being taught. In maths, she was able to socialise with so many of her friends and be herself, while simultaneously doing something she enjoyed, then she was miserable after the period ended. Science was used to give pep talks to herself on how to deal with Bryce, which hardly ever worked. PE was the most torturous thing ever, but at least Enola was able to relax her mind with an essay assigned by her English teacher. Now the question is if this will get better or not.

An Unfortunate Beginning

Nothing got better, but rather got worse. Enola was struggling to keep her boat afloat at school. She knew all the comments she was constantly receiving were projections of others' insecurities, but it happened so often that it was hard for her to accept that. Knowing Enola, she wouldn't tell a soul about what was happening to her.

Most people enjoy sleeping because it's a time to recharge and rest, but Enola valued sleeping because it was her escape from reality. At home, she dealt with high expectations to be just as perfect as her brother is, while also being a good role model for Avi while she is learning the ropes of life. She wanted time to stop. It was too hard for her to handle all of this stress. And what's worse is that no one she knew would understand her, not even

Nish. Kids at school viewed her as "the annoying kid" when she was just trying to fit in.

I hate to say this, but this escape of Enola's isn't going to last.

It was 2nd November, a day of celebration for Enola and Nish marking their one amazing year of friendship, when it all started. Enola went to school as normal with Nish, continuing to hide her emotions and keep them bottled up inside her, when Nish decided to conjure a plan. The two had been dealing with rumours about each other and were finding it difficult to hang out without someone making up a lie and spreading it like a disease. The plan was to ignore each other and be separate in hopes that the rumours would stop. Enola, reluctantly, agreed, unsure what to feel. She hated that she would have to ignore him on purpose, but at the same time, she knew that this change might be helpful. Even though she was keeping some distance from him, she still enjoyed having small conversations with him because, after all, they were still best friends.

That whole day was quite maddening. In French, she had completely bombed a weekly quiz they had and wasn't able to absorb any of the information being taught to her. In History, her teacher decided to go over the most uninteresting, to the point of sleepiness, topic in all of American history ever. Maths was a little better because she was able to do some fun, simple algebra while listening to Mrs Ahn's foolish humour, but still had to deal with her desk partner who wouldn't stop bugging her about her close friendship with Nish.

Then in Science, she died from boredom from an overly explained explanation of Newton's first law of motion. Fifth period was probably the worst of all six periods. Two jerks came up to her and decided to call attention to her acne. At this point, she was already used to being called names like "Pimple face", but occasionally it still hurts. Enola didn't even know the two people, yet they still felt the need to call her out.

She couldn't fathom how unbelievably horrible her day was going. After arriving to her sixth period with low hopes that this period might be any better, her English teacher decides to assign a five-page essay due in two days on the book the class was reading.

At this moment, Enola was simply fed up with life and would want nothing more than to be at home in fuzzy pyjamas with a teddy bear print all over them, and tucked tightly in her bed, sleeping. But of course, none of that was possible, because Enola would never have her greatly desired rest.

She went to bed that day, feeling like she was stuck in a never-ending cycle of frustration. Little did she know what was coming next.

Enola's Little Friend

Enola woke up on the cold floor in utter distress, sweat-soaked and disoriented, heart racing, gasping for breath as her eyes started to finally see her surroundings. Enola was no longer in her bedroom anymore. Tall, twisted trees loomed overhead, their branches intertwining like skeletal fingers, blocking out the moonlight. Enola, still a bit groggy, got up and began to walk around this unknown area. Breaking twigs fallen on the floor with each step, Enola could not make out where she was.

After a few minutes of walking around, her mind still adjusting to the unfamiliar scents, Enola approached the heart of the forest, where a hidden glade lay shrouded in twilight. The trees towered like ancient sentinels, their gnarled branches twisting towards the sky. A soft, ethereal glow emanated from the ground, where bioluminescent flowers bloomed. Their light flickered like stars, casting a gentle luminescence that danced upon the darkened path. Wisps of mist curled around the trunks, whispering secrets of enchantment. The air was thick with the scent of damp earth and wild herbs, while the distant sound of a bubbling brook added a melodic undertone, making the darkness feel alive with magic.

Enola was mesmerised by the beauty and peacefulness of the forest. She hadn't felt this feeling before. The feeling of soaring like a bird, unbound by any chains or barriers. She could just be herself, away from society, away from people who ruin her self-esteem, away from her misery.

Little did Enola know that this woodland was far from being tranquil, but was ironically known as "The Realm of Eternal Nightmares". She wandered the forest, admiring the serene surroundings with every step, completely oblivious to the sly fox deceptively gliding, and cunningly creeping through the shadows, following her.

After walking for a few minutes, she came across an illuminated cavern that was beyond beautiful. The cavern walls shimmered with a soft, golden glow, reflecting the light of countless glowing crystals embedded in the stone. Stalactites hung from the ceiling like chandeliers, each one glowing with a different colour, casting vibrant rainbows across the cavern. Her eyes sparkled like stars in the night sky, reflecting the shimmering silver surface of the pool of water in front of her from the peaceful waterfall that cascaded with a gentle flow from the roof of the cavern. Each glimmer seemed to hold a secret, as if the water was whispering tales of magic and wonder just for her.

Suddenly, the feeling of realisation struck her like a bolt of lightning, electrifying her head and making everything make sense. She was still dreaming. That realisation was far from true, but Enola didn't know any better. Besides seeing all of these glowing objects brightly lit up, she also saw an escape from the madness she was dealing with Winstoor.

Enola found a damp log inside the cavern on which she fell asleep. Little did she know the sharp-witted fox was hiding behind it, watching her. It swiftly hopped on the log and used its front two paws to shove Enola off the log.

"What was that?" Enola exclaimed in confusion. When she tilted her head back to the log, she saw the fox curled up tightly, tucking its bushy tail around its body, creating a warm, snug ball of fur. Its eyes were gently closed, and a relaxed expression was displayed across its face. Enola knew she couldn't shoo away the calm animal, so she decided to sleep on the floor.

But for some reason, Enola struggled to fall asleep, not because the floor was uncomfortable, but because her mind wouldn't stop thinking. She began to think about Nish, and her moving away from him. She couldn't help but think about how different life would be if she had just told him, if she hadn't distanced herself from him but lived her life more carefree, if she told him she didn't want to do the plan he created to stop the spread of the rumours. Before she knew it, she had begun to cry at the fact that she might have been happier if only she made some decisions differently.

The cute nestled fox had uncurled itself, seamlessly jumped off, and gently nuzzled its head into Enola's, its soft fur brushing against her forehead. With each nudge, a whimper escaped its lips, filled with worry and concern. It could sense that something was wrong, and its heart ached as it continued to nudge her, hoping for her to stop her sorrowful cries. With these small gestures, the little fox was trying to make sure that Enola was alright. For the rest of the night, the two were nestled together on the floor, falling asleep to the soothing sounds of water running into the tranquil pool at the base of the waterfall.

The First Encounter

Once, it was morning and Enola was quietly sleeping, the fox decided to take the task of waking her up. It carefully left its sleeping position and went outside to collect various wild berries growing on bushes right outside the cavern, some fallen twigs, and leaves. Once it had gathered all of its items, it headed back to the cavern, placed all of the berries on top of the leaves to protect them from the dirt on the ground, and put a twig in its mouth. With the stick, the fox gently poked her cheeks and brushed the stick through her tangled brown hair.

Enola is a very light sleeper, so she was awake from the moment the fox had woken up, but she pretended to stay asleep, curious about what the little fox was up to. To confuse the fox, she decided to shift her body, continuing to pretend that she was sleeping. Enola's silly plan had worked, because the fox had tilted its head, scurried over to the other side of Enola, and started poking her cheek once again. Enola wasn't budging, so the fox had to come up with a new plan. It nudged its wet snout into her cheek, hoping she would finally wake up, and this time she did. She got up, and with gentle hands, she stroked its silky orange fur, feeling the warmth radiate from its tiny body. The fox tilted its head, looking up at her with bright, intelligent eyes. She laughed as the fox playfully pawed at her fingers, its fluffy tail wagging happily. The fox suddenly ran to the leaves that had the berries and dragged them to Enola's feet.

Enola, shocked by what the fox had done, picked up the berries and started to brush off any dirt with her sleeve, and plop them in her mouth and occasionally the fox's. That's when Enola noticed something on the fox's neck. It was a collar with a name engraved on the front of it, and a different name on the back, along with an address.

"Amelia," read Enola, then she flipped over the collar to read the second name, "Dresden Gandalf, Aequcurin, Azadia. Hmm? Interesting name, I wonder who that is." Then she looked towards Amelia and introduced herself, "Hi Amelia, I'm Enola!"

After their brief introduction, Enola stepped out of the cavern, wanting to explore more of this magical place, but something had caught her eye and confused her tremendously.

She saw her house in the middle of the wilderness. With a puzzled look on her face, Enola sprinted to the house, hesitant to turn the doorknob, placed her hand on it and took a deep breath. Before she opened the door, she looked backwards, in search of Amelia, only to find her no longer there. At last, she shakily grasped it and rotated it. Inside, she saw her parents bringing huge brown cardboard boxes and putting in items like clothes, plates, and decorations. She saw her mum carefully folding clothes and stacking them into sturdy cardboard boxes, while her father would laugh as he discovered an old photo album, reminiscing about memories.

Her mother, who sensed Enola walking through the door with her mum-like-spidey-senses, abruptly said, "Hey darling, could you bring me the duct tape from the garage and a black Sharpie? I am almost done packing my clothes, so make sure you bring all your clothes from your dresser and into that box in the corner next to the TV." Enola stared blankly at her mother, confused as to why everyone was packing their things. It was nowhere near March 9th, the day they were actually meant to start moving.

Trying to connect the dots and figure out where the puzzle pieces went, Enola, with slight hope she wouldn't give her the answer that would crush her, decided to ask, "Mum, what day is today?"

With a slight chuckle, her mum replied, "It's March 9th, you know, the big day!"

That singular reply made Enola's heart sink. The day she had been dreading for months had arrived and left her in utter despair. Tears began to well up in her eyes as she tried to convince herself that none of this was happening. She felt the weight of the world pressing down on her chest, making it hard to breathe, and she feared that everything around her was crumbling. She could no longer hold back her feelings and collapsed on the floor and covered her face with both of her palms.

Her mum rushed to her to comfort her, and wrapped her arms around her, confused as to what was happening. After releasing a pond's worth of tears, Enola finally said, "I don't want to move, Mum, I don't want to move. I won't be able to make new friends. Please can we not move, please."

Enola's mum, trying to understand Enola's concerns, knew it was too late to make any changes. She was aware that Enola wasn't happy about them moving, but she didn't realise how much she despised this new change, or how much it would affect her.

In an attempt to break the news to Enola, her mother used a very calm and soft voice to tell her, "Enola, sweetie, it's far too late to cancel everything. We have already bought the house and ordered two moving trucks. Now I know you don't approve of this, and I understand that change is hard, but we have to do this. There will be better opportunities for you in Westbrook and we will build a better future for you. And believe me when I say this, you will have no trouble finding new friends. You have a beautiful personality, like a ray of warm sunshine on a cold day, spreading kindness and positivity to everyone around you, and a heart full of empathy and love. What more could one want in a friend than that? I know this will be hard, but I believe in you."

It had been a while since Enola had had someone say something like that to her. She was just getting used to people bullying her about the way that she looked and how she acted in front of others, and she found it hard to believe her mother. Although she was moved by her mother's uplifting words, she couldn't help but think of her friends, and everyone she was leaving behind in this new chapter of her life.

Unfortunately, things were about to get worse from here.

What is Happening?

Suddenly, Enola, still in her mother's arms, felt the ground start to rumble. Enola's mother didn't seem to notice this happening as she continued to comfort her, while Enola was as puzzled as a cat in a dog park. The rumbling got more violent each second, and every object had started to levitate, and gold dust filled the room. With a blink of an eye, Enola's house was no longer there, and the woodlands were nowhere to be seen.

All that could be seen was a junior high school that Enola recognised because it was the school she went to. The school is surrounded by tall trees and colourful flower gardens, creating a peaceful atmosphere. Inside the school, the walls are decorated with student artwork and posters showcasing upcoming events. Through the glass windows, you could see bright classrooms filled with inspiring quotes and learning materials, making it a vibrant place to learn. As Enola was walking through the school, she saw someone she thought she would never see again. It was Nish! Although he was walking with his head down and looked extremely depressed, that didn't stop Enola from bolting to him at full speed, screaming his name, so grateful to see him again after all that she had been through. Usually, Nish is extremely attentive and always aware whenever Enola is with him. However, this was different and odd. He didn't even acknowledge her as she was speaking to him but continued to look down at the floor.

Enola and Nish have a daily routine of lightly tapping each other on their heads, usually done to get each other's attention or just to annoy them for their amusement. Enola thought that if she bonked him on his head, he would finally notice her walking beside him. Except she couldn't tap him, because her hand had gone through his head like a hologram. The amount of confusion about Enola is indescribable. Nothing was making sense. One minute, she was just lying on her bed and woke up to find herself in a deserted forest, and the next minute she was in her school, filled with hologram images of her friends.

Not only was Enola tremendously confused, but she felt a wave of emotions over her that she couldn't control. Why was she provoked from speaking with her best friend? She couldn't help feeling guilty and sad because of how Nish was acting. He was the most joyful person Enola knew. Whenever Enola had gotten a bad grade or was emotionally hurt by all the comments she was receiving, Nish was the one there to comfort her and always made sure she understood that all the comments others were telling her were utter lies. And now that he is hurt, she can't do anything about it. Enola was on the verge of crying another pond when she felt a tap on the shoulder.

She turned around to see none other than Jordan, better known as Jigsaw, as he accidentally swallowed a puzzle piece when he was eight years old. Jordan has never been the brightest and would often fail homework assignments. One thing he did excel in was ruining someone's day, or in this case, making Enola's day worse than it already was to begin with.

"Yo Enola," began talking Jordan in his annoying, extremely high-pitched voice, one resembling a mouse, "You should go wash your face to clean off your pimples." Enola has never received a dumber request than that and responded with, "That's not how acne works, you do know that, right?" Under her breath, she muttered, "But of course you wouldn't know that because you don't know anything."

Jordan, hoping that Enola would burst out crying, decided to say another insult to hopefully demolish her confidence, "What do you mean that's not how it works? Just wash your face, it's not that hard. And while you're at it, maybe use some make-up, because with and without your acne, you're still ugly. Hopefully, make-up can help."

Enola was no longer going to stay strong and let others treat her like this. She clenched her fists as her face reddened with anger. Without any hesitation whatsoever, Enola threw her fist into Jordan's eye, similar to what Nish had done to Bryce, except twenty times harder. All her life, Enola has been treated unfairly and would never do anything to stop it but would rather allow it to happen to her. But Enola didn't stop there. Enola had hit him so hard that he fell backwards to the ground, screaming in pain, and while on the floor, Enola kicked his side, bruising it badly.

If the boy from behind Enola had not pushed her away from the boy, she would've broken every bone in his body. Enola struggled to escape the captives she was put in and tried running out. Suddenly, Nish, who had provoked Enola to hurt Jordan even more, pulled her closer to him and tightly hugged her, hoping to calm her down. It took about ten minutes for Enola to calm down and come back to her senses. When she was finally calm, she collapsed down to her knees, her eyes filled with tears. Why couldn't people be nice to her, even if it was just for a day? Enola has tried so hard to change, to be someone people might like, but they never gave her a second chance.

Whenever Enola is in distress, like now, Nish always tries to use a soothing voice to make sure she doesn't lash out at him or anyone else, because once Enola has reached her peak anger, she becomes unpredictable. For example, she would never hit another person, but with all her anger bottled up for years, she hit him out of instinct. Nish, trying not to upset Enola even more, said softly, "Enola, are you okay?"

He knew it was obvious that she wasn't, but he didn't know what else to say. Enola turned around and faced him, tears rushing down her cheek. Without any hesitation, Nish took her into his arms and let her cry on his shoulder. He knew she had gone through a lot, and he knew that he needed to be the one to make her feel better.

Please Stop, Please Stop

The ground began to shake once again, and everything had disappeared like a blur, including Nish. In the blink of an eye, Enola was in a place she had never seen before. There were bustling streets that surrounded, and the giggles and laughter of students were all that could be heard, besides the occasional honk of horns at rash drivers. Enola found herself sitting in the middle of a field of grass, staring at the groups of children playing around her. She could tell she was at a school of some sort, and she had this fuzzy memory of getting on a flight with her parents and moving into their new house. As she thought about it more, she was able to put together the puzzle pieces. She was no longer in Winstoor. Enola's heart sank to the floor. She had no idea what was happening to her, but realised that she was miles away from everybody she knew.

She decided to get up from the slightly wet grass and approach a group of girls who were doing gymnastic tricks. She tapped one girl with extremely curly brown hair that was tied in a loose ponytail with a white scrunchie that complimented her outfit.

“Um, excuse me, do you think I could join you guys? I am sort of alone.”

The young girl turned around and replied with an extremely confused expression on her face, “Uh, who even are you?”

“I am Enola. I just moved here from Winstoor.” “So you’re the new kid, huh? I honestly thought you were going to look totally different.”

“Oh,” replied Enola, unsure what to say to that. “Anyways, what was your question again?”

“I was just wondering if I could possibly join you guys?”

“You want to join us?”

“Uh, yes?” Enola said, with a slight confusion in her voice.
The girl laughed a little and replied, “Um, I don't think you understand, but we can never be seen with someone like… you. You are simply too weird for our standards.” “Oh, sorry to disturb you. I’ll just leave now,” said Enola, with a break in her voice.

“As you should,” replied the girl, and turned her back towards Enola and continued talking with her friends. Enola had low hopes of making friends in this school. She walked away from the group and decided to explore the school she was going to be held captive in for the rest of the day. Enola noticed how vibrant and colourful the walls of this new school were. There were murals everywhere sending out positive messages; however, the students here didn't seem to acknowledge them, hence their behaviour. Enola, more depressed than before, started walking on the blacktop, looking down and being completely clueless about her surroundings, that she didn't hear a young boy scream, "GET OUT OF THE WAY," as a bouncy ball came flying and hit her head, which knocked her out. She fell to the ground, and the boy who had screamed had rushed to her. Enola's vision was extremely blurry and there was a faint ringing sound. The young boy was asking her if she was alright, but with the ringing sound, she could hardly hear a word he said. Some other students who had witnessed this had also eventually come to her, while others had requested an adult on sight to assist Enola with her injury. She was brought to her feet by two girls who assisted her when going to the nurse's office. Nurses in this district weren't known for being effective in treating patients, so all the nurse did was ask her if she needed an ice pack for her head. Enola had figured that this nightmare was never going to end, so she decided to toughen up and tell the nurse she was OK. As she was walking back, her hand on her head hoping that would help the pain go away, she heard the bell ring. All of the fuzzy memories Enola had of this place were gone, and Enola was lost in the middle of the school, without a clue of where to go and which classroom she belonged to. The closest classroom near her was room 410, and she saw kids that looked around her age, so she quickly slipped in. She waited for everyone to sit down and found an empty seat at the back of the classroom, next to two girls who were sneakily doing their makeup in class. She saw on the right side of the board an organised schedule, with one hour per subject. At the top left corner was written the teacher's name: Mrs Allblue.

As Enola was looking around the classroom, admiring all the decorations hung on the doors, she saw some students whispering into each other's ears and pointing at her. She couldn't help but start to feel worse about her appearance. She was almost certain they were whispering about her acne, height, or the clothes she was wearing, which were the usual topics she got bullied on at her old school. Soon the whispering turned into laughing, indicating that Enola's assumptions were right after all. Enola couldn't take it anymore, and she sprinted away from the school. She hoped that everything there would be different, that people could finally treat her properly like a real human being and not someone that could be taken advantage of. So, she ran. Running away from one's problems is never the solution, and Enola knew this, but running helped her cool off. She had no idea where she was going, but she ran out of school bounds and onto the streets. Enola has always been able to run extremely fast for long distances when she's angry, which was the emotion that currently took over her state of mind. While running around this foreign area, Enola ignored all traffic laws and just sprinted in the same direction. Cars were continuously honking at her, and drivers would stick their heads out of the driver's seat window to yell at her, but that didn't stop Enola.

Enola was running through all the traffic, dodging all the cars that wanted to cross the intersection but had to quickly press their brakes. However, some drivers were not the most attentive, and one of them had not seen Enola running through the middle of the road. The driver braked too soon, and Enola toppled over the car and hit the windshield. Enola, still blinded by fury, decided to slide off the car, hastily apologised to the driver, who was out of their car wanting to make sure Enola was alright, and proceeded to run in the same direction. As she was running, she thought of her name and how unusual it was. In her mind, she rearranged the letters, seeing if any words could be made. It was at this moment Enola realised that her name backwards spelled out "Alone". Enola truly was alone. But Enola didn't stop running. She ran through a park, when all of a sudden, the scenery in front of her began to change like a glitch, and she was no longer in her new city.

Goodbye Enola

Enola just wanted everything to end. She didn't know what was happening to her. She was just sleeping in her own room, and now she was travelling all over the place, dealing with more sadness than the encounters before. When the ground began shaking again, she knew she was going to be transported once again, and felt worse than before.

To her surprise, Enola was back in the woodlands where she met Amelia and found her house behind the cavern. Except the cavern was no longer there, but rather a village. Now, you may remember the slight mention of a village from the first chapter, but much happened before the monster was introduced.

Amelia had rushed to Enola when she saw her, nudged its head into her ankle, and began to purr. The simple gesture had made Enola feel much better about the abominably frightening chain of happenings that had just unfolded. It made her remember her mother's words, and perhaps the last words she would ever hear from her mother.

Although Enola was back in the same woodlands, something had changed. The trees were dressed in vibrant shades of red, orange, and gold; the feeling of crunching leaves beneath your feet, the crisp air that carries the scent of pine and earth, and children playing in the piles of fallen leaves, leaving the sound of laughter all throughout the air.

She noticed some villagers sharpening some of their obsidian tools with some sandpaper, and cleaning up the edges with the tip of a deer's antler, and chopping some wood with an axe to make bows and arrows. Enola had been so used to seeing everything machine-made that she had never seen the process of someone making anything by hand. She was simply amazed and awestruck. It had been a while since she had seen everyone working together. Everyone was happy, and they weren't judging each other.

Once the villagers had noticed her, instead of seeing her as a potential enemy, they welcomed her with open arms, and began to sing a welcome song in their native language. Enola had never felt so accepted in her life. Everyone at school saw her as someone who didn't belong. At home, she had to always be a good role model, which meant being someone she wasn't. But here, she could just be Enola.

Amapoloa, the head chief of the village, had greeted her as if she was one of his people, and treated her as if they had known her forever.

Then there was a loud shriek coming from the back of one of the huts. One of the mothers had been violently murdered. Next thing you know, half of the village is being slaughtered by this wild, ugly beast, clawing its victims and leaving no remorse. Enola had a feeling that the monster making an appearance was no coincidence. To save the rest of the villagers, she decided to sacrifice herself and gather all of the beast's attention towards her. With this distraction, all of the remaining survivors went into hiding, waiting for the perfect moment to strike the beast dead.

Enola started to create a pile of fallen sticks and began throwing them at the filthy beast. This was the moment Enola realised just how large the creature actually was, and her legs had stopped responding, which led to her falling down in fear. To instil more fear into Enola, the monster had grabbed a severely wounded villager from the floor and slaughtered them right in front of Enola's eyes.

She was trembling; her hands were shaking vigorously. She couldn't believe her eyes, nor comprehend the series of events that took place. Her mind had drawn to a blank, and there was a tremendous amount of terror visible in her eyes. Her breaths started getting louder and heavier with each exhale. She knew she had to run away from the horror, but her legs weren't obeying her mind. To pause for a moment here, if you read back to the first chapter, you may recognise this paragraph, but never found out what happened afterwards. So, in case you have forgotten the series of events, I will restate them for you. The monster, with blood smeared all over its face and claws, had approached the young girl, eyes filled with fearsome menace. Even after going on a murderous rampage, the wild beast still had a voracious appetite for more. What more could it possibly want? It slowly came closer to Enola, licking the blood off its knife-like claws. Although Enola was unable to run away to potentially save her life, she was able to scoot herself backward just a couple of feet. Enola was on the verge of accepting that her life was going to end at any moment, when suddenly, she heard a swift movement from behind the monster. The monster and Enola broke their gaze as the beast turned back. There was nothing, just pitch silence. But of course, the ignorant beast took a few steps in the direction of the noise. After turning its neck left and right sharply, almost like how mums make kids do before crossing a road, the monster concluded there was nothing there. It had completely ignored the broken twigs on the floor, and a villager's head peeking out from one of the trees. Moments later, there was an attack. Villagers, who had climbed high on the sequoia trees, jumped down on the wretched creature, stabbing it with freshly sharpened arrowheads made out of obsidian. The villagers, completely unaware that this creature had been alive for over 1,000 years and would not be affected by a stab wound, continued to attack the creature. Enola took advantage of the distraction, got up, and started running. She looked at Amapoloa, who had given her a slight nod of approval to run away. She ran as fast as she could, faster than ever before. The poor, unfortunate villagers had misjudged the beast, because seconds later, after the attack, the beast had aggressively shaken off all the people from his bulky back and thrown them to the ground.

Once it saw that Enola was no longer on the floor, which was covered in withered sepia leaves, it grunted in frustration that it had lost its prey, and decided to walk slowly, inspecting every direction for a sign that the girl may still be nearby. Enola, still running, looked back occasionally to see if the ugly monster was in hindsight. It wasn't. She took a well-deserved break, rested her back against a tree, and took deep and heavy breaths. She took advantage of this moment to recollect her thoughts. So much had happened to her, and the thirst for water was much desired, but in a forest with little to no streams, this was difficult to acquire.

Suddenly, Enola heard a noise, a noise she recognised very well, a faint growl. It sounded like a lion when it came into close contact with a deer. Instantly, it clicked. She knew what had just approached her. She took a deep sigh, accepting her fate, and fearfully looked up. It was the beast, its beady eyes staring straight at her. It took a great leap, claws in the air, mouth open to devour, with a stance of each limb opened wide, and slaughtered her torso and left her to bleed out. Purple fog then hovered over the monster, and just like that, it had disappeared.

All of the villagers who were alive rushed to aid her, hoping she could survive. Half of the survivors were picking up her dead body and bringing it to a hut they used as their hospital, while the other half were collecting ingredients that could help her recover. As everyone was rushing, knowing that Enola had very little time left to have a chance of surviving, a crow swooped down from its nest and was perched on the top of the hospital hut, staring at everyone working as fast as they could. Enola didn't make it.

Reflection

I chose this as my strongest piece of writing in my novel because I have included many sensory details in hopes that the reader will envision the same thing I was envisioning. Although it has quite a tragic end, it holds great meaning as well. I think, deep down, everyone has a monster hidden inside them, and no one is purely good. I have included this segment in my story because I want to convey the message that Enola is fighting her inner demons, with all the negativity brought to her by others from her school. However, Enola is fighting a real-life demon. I was hoping to convey the message that life is not always happy and that it gets challenging to deal with, and I feel that I have accomplished that well. Many stories often end in happy endings, but not everyone is dealt a good life. In conclusion, I think this passage is very detailed and quite meaningful.

I Apologise

Now I don't quite know how to tell you this lightly, but I want you to know before I say it that it was a very honest mistake, and I didn't mean it. Unfortunately, it was me who had cursed Enola. I did not do this on purpose; I wasn't even aware of who Enola was. Due to the frustration, I was experiencing, I must have said the spell wrong and said *Enolakim* instead of *Englokim*. Now you may be wondering why I did not do anything to prevent all the horrible things Enola had to face. Well, the spell I cast was irreversible, so whatever happened to Enola next was simply out of my control. I tried everything in my power to try to find a way to help her, whether it was joining her in her nightmare, or a way to wake her up. But the spell was far too strong. All I could do was watch her suffer through my mirror.

As soon as I realised what I had done, I began to flip through the ancient spell book that I was not allowed to have, in hope of finding some sort of spell to perhaps lessen the pain and suffering. Eventually, I found something that might do the trick. Hesitant to cast the spell, I grabbed the stolen wand and began to enchant the incantation, and flicked my wrist in the appropriate ways for the spell to work.

"Extiaro," Right flick! "Obliegris," Upward flick!

"Canierous," Left flick!

I'm really sorry for this, but once Enola returned to the woodlands, I had to cast that spell to send the monster to attack her. The monster's only job was to take Enola's life, but it is a wild beast, so the death of the other villagers was out of my hands. I couldn't bear seeing Enola suffer for so long when her life was already torturous to begin with. To end Enola's excruciating pain, I had to cast the spell. It was the only way. I had to... I had to take her life.

My heart ached at the sight of Enola's sorrow; it was like a heavy weight on my chest, suffocating me. It was the only way. I hope she is in a better, more peaceful place. She finally received the escape she always wanted, only that was forever.

www.ingramcontent.com/pod-product-compliance
Ingram Content Group UK Ltd.
Pitfield, Milton Keynes, MK11 3LW, UK
UKHW041311190726
13845UKWH00025B/201

9 789364 020664